HELLO KITTY®
and
♥ME♥

Bedtime

SANRIO, HELLO KITTY and associated logos are trademarks
and/or registered trademarks of Sanrio Co., Ltd.
©1976, 2014 SANRIO CO., LTD.

Copyright © 2014 by Sanrio Co., Ltd.
Cover and internal design © 2014 by Sourcebooks, Inc.
Cover design by Randee Ladden and Brittany Vibbert
Text by Jacqueline A. Ball
Internal design by Angela Navarra

Sourcebooks and the colophon are registered trademarks of Sourcebooks, Inc.

Published by Sourcebooks Jabberwocky, an imprint of Sourcebooks, Inc.
P.O. Box 4410, Naperville, Illinois 60567-4410
(630) 961-3900
Fax: (630) 961-2168
www.jabberwockykids.com

Library of Congress Cataloging-in-Publication data is on file with the publisher.

Source of Production: Worzalla, Stevens Point WI, USA
Date of Production: August 2014
Run Number: 5002115

Printed and bound in the United States of America.
WOZ 10 9 8 7 6 5 4 3 2 1

Hello Kitty and her friends played in the park all afternoon.

Now everyone is going home for dinner.

See you tomorrow!

All that fun in the park made
Hello Kitty very tired.

It's time to get ready for bed.

Every night, Hello Kitty likes to do special things before bed.

Come along and help!

First, Hello Kitty likes to take a nice warm bath with her yellow duckie.

But wait! Where's her duckie?

Then she dries herself off with
a fluffy towel.

Can you count the hearts on Hello Kitty's pajamas?

She puts on her pajamas and
brushes her teeth.
But now she has lost a slipper!

Do you see Hello Kitty's other slipper?

Every night, Hello Kitty looks at the stars. Then she makes a wish.

What's your wish tonight?

Mama is ready to read a bedtime story. But Hello Kitty wants to play.

**Hello Kitty loves playing
hide-and-seek. Can you find her?**

There's Hello Kitty!

Now she's ready for Mama to read her favorite storybook.

Hello Kitty is so sleepy! Mama gives her a kiss.

Papa comes in to give her a hug.

Good night, Hello Kitty! Sleep tight! The stars will shine on you tonight.

Hello Kitty snuggles with her bedtime friends so they will feel safe and cozy.

What kinds of stuffed animals does Hello Kitty have?

Soon, Hello Kitty is asleep.
She dreams about all her friends.

Then she dreams about the fun they will have tomorrow.

Sweet dreams,
Hello Kitty!